THE HISTORY OF THE NEW ENGLAND PATRIOTS

Published by Creative Education
123 South Broad Street
Mankato, Minnesota 56001
Creative Education is an imprint of The Creative Company.

DESIGN AND PRODUCTION BY **EVANSDAY DESIGN**

LIBRARY OF CONGRESS CATALOGING-IN-PUBLICATION DATA

Bell, Lonnie.
The history of the New England Patriots / by Lonnie Bell.
p. cm. — (NFL today)
Summary: Traces the history of the team from its beginnings through 2003.
ISBN 1-58341-304-9
1. New England Patriots (Football team)—History—Juvenile literature.
[1. New England Patriots (Football team)—History.
2. Football—History.] I. Title. II. Series.

GV956.N36B45 2004
796.332'64'0974461—dc22   2003062579

First edition

9 8 7 6 5 4 3 2 1

COVER PHOTO: defensive tackle Richard Seymour

PATRIOTS

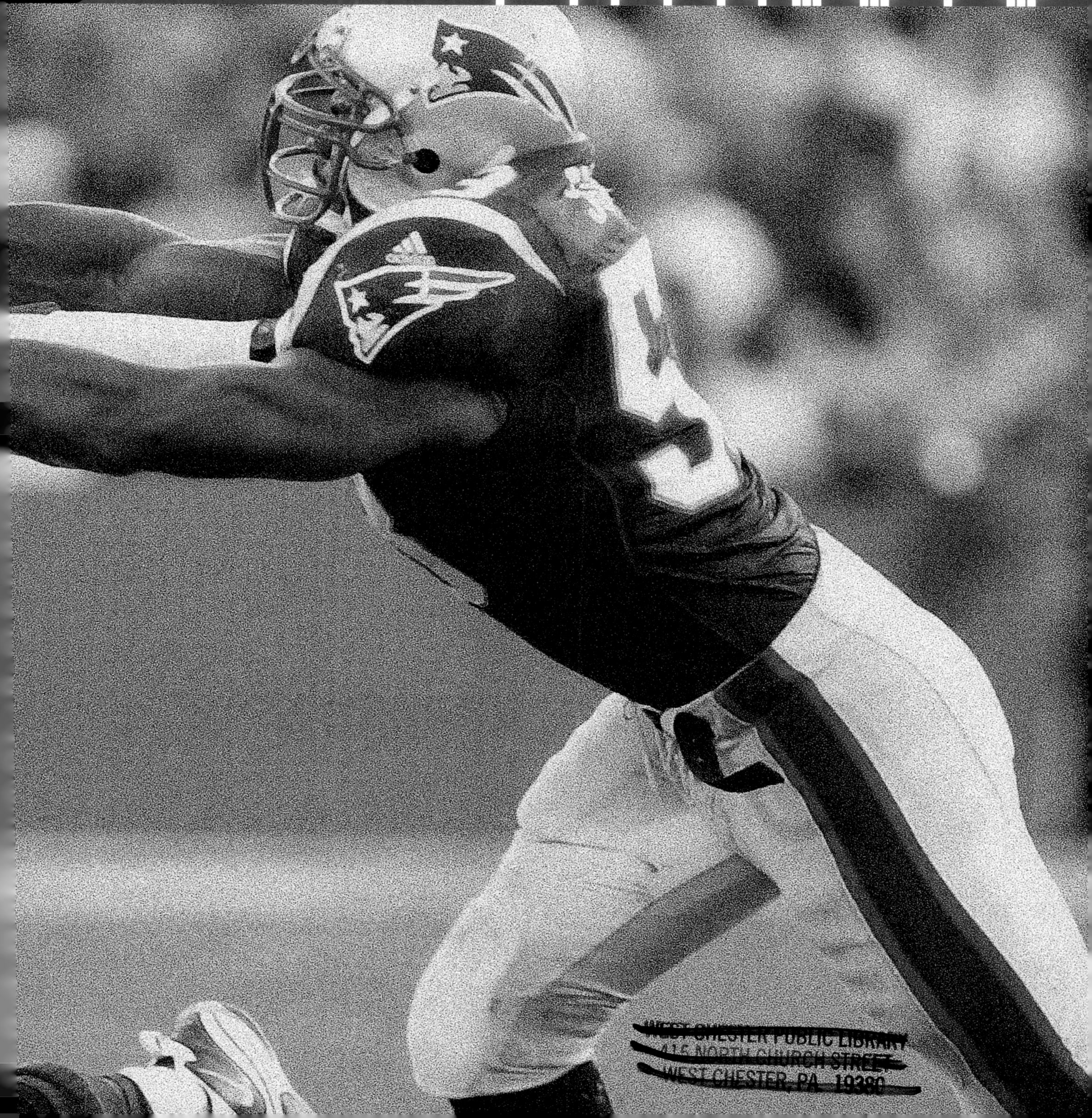

IN 1620, ENGLISH COLONISTS CALLED PILGRIMS SAILED FROM ENGLAND TO THE ROCKY COAST OF WHAT WOULD LATER BECOME THE NORTHEASTERN UNITED STATES. THEY NAMED THE AREA WHERE THEY SETTLED NEW ENGLAND. AT FIRST, NEW ENGLANDERS WERE RULED BY GREAT BRITAIN, BUT BY 1775 MANY OF THEM WANTED TO GOVERN THEMSELVES. THESE PEOPLE—WHO WERE CALLED PATRIOTS—FOUGHT FOR THEIR FREEDOM IN THE AMERICAN REVOLUTIONARY WAR.

TODAY, NEW ENGLAND INCLUDES THE STATES OF CONNECTICUT, MAINE, MASSACHUSETTS, NEW HAMPSHIRE, RHODE ISLAND, AND VERMONT. AND IT'S STILL HOME TO PATRIOTS—THE NEW ENGLAND PATRIOTS PROFESSIONAL FOOTBALL TEAM, THAT IS. THESE GRIDIRON WARRIORS ARE NOT FIGHTING THE BRITISH, THOUGH. SINCE 1970, THEY'VE BEEN BATTLING TO BE THE TOP TEAM IN THE NATIONAL FOOTBALL LEAGUE (NFL).

[1984 New England Patriots]

THE PATRIOTS WERE formed in 1960 as part of a

new league called the American Football League (AFL).

Originally known as the Boston Patriots (since the team

was based in Boston, Massachusetts), they featured a

number of fine players. This included quarterback Babe

Parilli, defensive tackle Jim Lee "Earthquake" Hunt, and

defensive end Bob Dee, who scored the first touchdown

in AFL history on a fumble recovery.

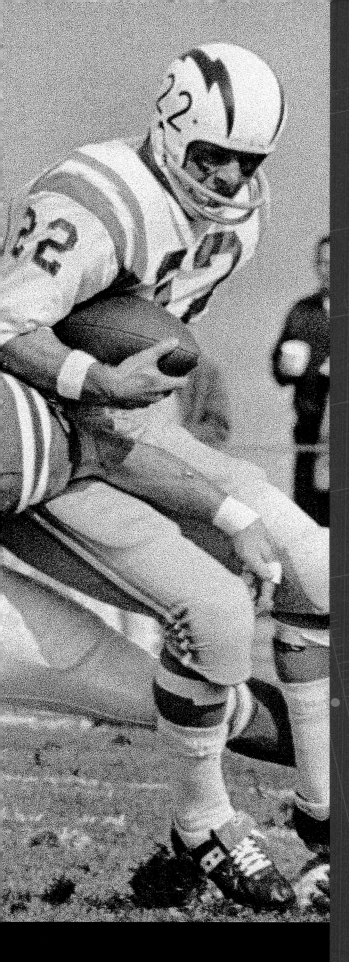

Also starting in those early years were Gino Cappelletti and Nick Buoniconti. Cappelletti was a versatile athlete who played both wide receiver and kicker and put together two of the top five scoring seasons in AFL history (147 points in 1961 and 155 points in 1964). Buoniconti, meanwhile, was a steely linebacker who stood only 5-foot-11 but was famous for his toughness and nonstop motor. "If you are lucky enough to knock him down," Kansas City Chiefs quarterback Len Dawson once said of Buoniconti, "you have to lay on him or he'll get right back into the play."

These players made the Patriots one of the AFL's strongest teams in the early 1960s. Boston put together a winning record in four of its first five years. In 1963, the Patriots went 7–6–1, then whipped the Buffalo Bills 26–8 in the playoffs to advance to the AFL championship game. Unfortunately, they faced the powerful San Diego Chargers, who crushed them 51–10. Patriots fans didn't know it yet, but it would be 22 years before their team would again reach a league championship game.

IN 1965, THE PATRIOTS welcomed a new star: running back Jim Nance. When Nance arrived at training camp before the season, it was clear why he was nicknamed "Big Bo." At 260 pounds, he was heavier than most of the team's linemen. A year later, Nance reported to training camp at a trim 235 pounds and tore through opposing defenses for an AFL-record 1,458 rushing yards.

Nance made a practice of running over—not around—defenders, and he quickly became one of the AFL's most feared runners. "I've been noticing that when a guy hits me head-on, he's not quite so quick to hit me the next time," Nance said. "So I keep running at him, and pretty soon he wants to turn his shoulder. Then I know I've got him. When a man turns his shoulder on me, I'm going to get past him before he turns back."

Andre Tippett (pictured) followed in the footsteps of Nick Buoniconti as a star New England linebacker^

Despite the offensive heroics of Nance and Cappelletti, and the aggressive play of defensive tackle Houston Antwine, the Patriots fell to the bottom of the AFL standings in the late 1960s. Boston became notorious for its poor fan attendance, which was so low that the team hadn't even invested in a permanent home. By the time the AFL and NFL merged into one league in 1970, the Patriots had called five different fields home in their first 10 years.

In 1971, the team finally adopted Schaefer Stadium in Foxboro, Massachusetts, as its home field. To better reflect the team's new location on the outskirts of Boston, team owner Billy Sullivan changed its name to the New England Patriots.

THROUGHOUT THE 1970S, the Patriots added several players who would make them winners again. The first of these additions was guard John Hannah, who was drafted out of the University of Alabama in 1973. Known to his teammates as "Hog," the 6-foot-3 and 265-pound Hannah dominated opponents with his incredible strength and intensity. "He played first string from the day we got him," said Ron Erhardt, who was the team's head coach in the late 1970s. "With his attitude, John Hannah could play if he had been 5-foot-2."

After a discouraging 3–11 finish in 1975, the Patriots put their sputtering offense in the hands of backup quarterback Steve Grogan. Although he had a strong arm, Grogan was perhaps better known for his scrambling ability and willingness to take big hits. "He's our leader, our motivator...," said Hannah. "There are only a few quarterbacks

Tough quarterback Steve Grogan led the Patriots in passing for 11 seasons in the 1970s and '80s

who will do what Steve does now. He'll sit there, hold the ball, he'll get that lick, and then throw. It makes you want to give up a little bit of your life for him."

With Grogan leading an offense that also featured fullback Sam Cunningham—and with rookie cornerback Mike Haynes and end Tony McGee anchoring a solid defense—the 1976 Patriots jumped to an 11–3 record. Although the fairy tale season came to an end with a heartbreaking, 24–21 playoff loss to the mighty Oakland Raiders, New England fans were sure their Patriots were ready to take the next step.

Unfortunately, the Patriots could not quite reach the top of the NFL mountain. They put together winning records the next four seasons and returned to the playoffs in 1978, but a Super Bowl remained just a dream. Those years were also marred by a sad incident. In a preseason game in 1978, Patriots receiver Darryl Stingley broke his neck going for a pass and was paralyzed. After this tragedy, New England slid back down the standings, going 2–14 in 1981.

Linebacker Tedy Bruschi (pictured) played with a toughness that reminded fans of such former greats as John Hannah.^

THE PATRIOTS' SWOON did not last long, though, as more talent continued to arrive. In 1982, New England added young linebacker Andre Tippett through the NFL Draft. A year later, the Patriots found a quality backup for Steve Grogan by drafting a speedy quarterback named Tony Eason.

With these players lined up alongside the likes of Grogan and Hannah, the Patriots went 11–5 in 1985 and made the playoffs. Head coach Raymond Berry, who wanted to emphasize a running attack, made Eason his starting quarterback in the playoffs. Eason mainly handed the ball off to running back Craig James as the Patriots disposed of one opponent after another. Incredibly, after beating the New York Jets (26–14), Los Angeles Raiders (27–20), and Miami Dolphins (31–14), the Patriots headed to the Super Bowl to take on the Chicago Bears.

In his first season as the team's starting quarterback (1984), Tony Eason tossed 23 touchdown passes

John Stephens was named to the 1988 Pro Bowl after adding 1,168 yards to the Patriots' ground attack^

New England started strong against Chicago, kicking a field goal barely a minute into the game for the fastest score in Super Bowl history. But the powerful Bears then took over, scoring the next 44 points on their way to a 46–10 rout. Patriots fans were disappointed with the outcome but proud of their team, which had come just one victory away from a world championship.

In 1986, New England got a boost from wide receiver Stanley "Steamer" Morgan. Morgan had made two trips to the Pro Bowl in the early '80s before falling into a slump. But in 1986, he reported to training camp in great shape and had the best season of his Patriots career, setting team records with 84 catches for 1,491 yards. "I got lazy and got into some bad habits [before]," he said. "Now, I'm excited about playing football again."

The 1986 Patriots made the playoffs behind Morgan's great efforts, but they were quickly beaten. With the help of running back John Stephens and linebacker Johnny Rembert, New England remained a strong team the next two seasons as well. But in 1989, the Patriots dropped to 5–11. Three more losing seasons followed, and by 1993, the Patriots and their fans were looking for a hero to put the team back on the winning track.

NEW ENGLAND FOUND that hero in former New York Giants coach Bill Parcells, who was hired as the Patriots' head coach in 1993. One of Parcells's first moves was to use the team's top pick in the 1993 NFL Draft to select Drew Bledsoe, a 6-foot-5 quarterback out of Washington State University. Bledsoe was known both for his strong arm and his coolness under pressure, and he quickly became a star. In 1994, the 22-year-old threw for 4,555 yards—one of the highest totals in NFL history—and became the youngest quarterback ever elected to the Pro Bowl.

Led by the cool Bledsoe and fiery Parcells, the Patriots went 10–6 in 1994 and returned to the playoffs. Things got even better two years later. By then, the team was loaded with talented offensive players such as running back Curtis Martin, tight end Ben Coates, and tackle Bruce Armstrong.

With Coach Parcells driving these players, New England jumped to 11–5 and won the American Football Conference (AFC) Eastern Division.

In New England's first-ever home playoff game victory, the Patriots crushed the Pittsburgh Steelers 28–3. They then beat the Jacksonville Jaguars 20–6 to capture the AFC championship and make their second trip to the Super Bowl. New England's opponent in the 1996 Super Bowl was the Green Bay Packers. The first quarter was a showcase of offensive power, as the teams combined for 24 points. From there, however, the Packers pulled away to win 35–21.

New England fans were left even more disappointed after the loss when Parcells left town. Bledsoe, safety Lawyer Milloy, and cornerback Ty Law kept the Patriots among the AFC's best teams in the late 1990s, but they could not earn another shot at the Super Bowl.

IN 2000, THE Patriots hired Bill Belichick—a former Parcells assistant known for his brilliant defensive strategies—as their new head coach. Coach Belichick's first season in New England produced a meager 5–11 record. But 2001 turned out to be a season to remember.

When Bledsoe was injured in 2001, Belichick turned to young backup quarterback Tom Brady. Although the 24-year-old had previously thrown only three NFL passes, he had a swaggering style about him and was known to offer advice to his more experienced teammates. One Patriots coach later recalled thinking, "If he's this confident as a backup, I can only imagine how he'd be running the show."

With Brady running the show, New England started out just 1–3. But once he got comfortable and began to connect with wide receiver Troy Brown, the Patriots started to roll. By the end of the season, they were 11–5 and champions of the AFC East. In a snowy playoff matchup, the Patriots came from behind to beat the Oakland Raiders 16–13 in overtime. A week later, New England beat the Pittsburgh Steelers 24–17 to advance to the Super Bowl.

Opposing the Patriots in the Super Bowl were the St. Louis Rams, whose offense was so powerful that oddsmakers made them 14-point favorites to win. But behind Brady's cool play and a frenzied defensive effort, the Patriots jumped out to a surprising 17–3 lead. The Rams fought back to tie the game at 17–17, but with just seconds left on the clock, Patriots kicker Adam Vinatieri booted a 48-yard field goal to give New England its first world championship. Two days later, more than one million jubilant fans gathered at a celebratory rally in Boston to welcome the Patriots home. "Well," Brady said, "we've got a whole team full of underdogs, and now we're the top dogs!"

In 2002, the Patriots moved into the new, 68,000-seat Gillette Stadium. Although they fell short of the playoffs that year, they came back stronger than ever in 2003. Bledsoe had

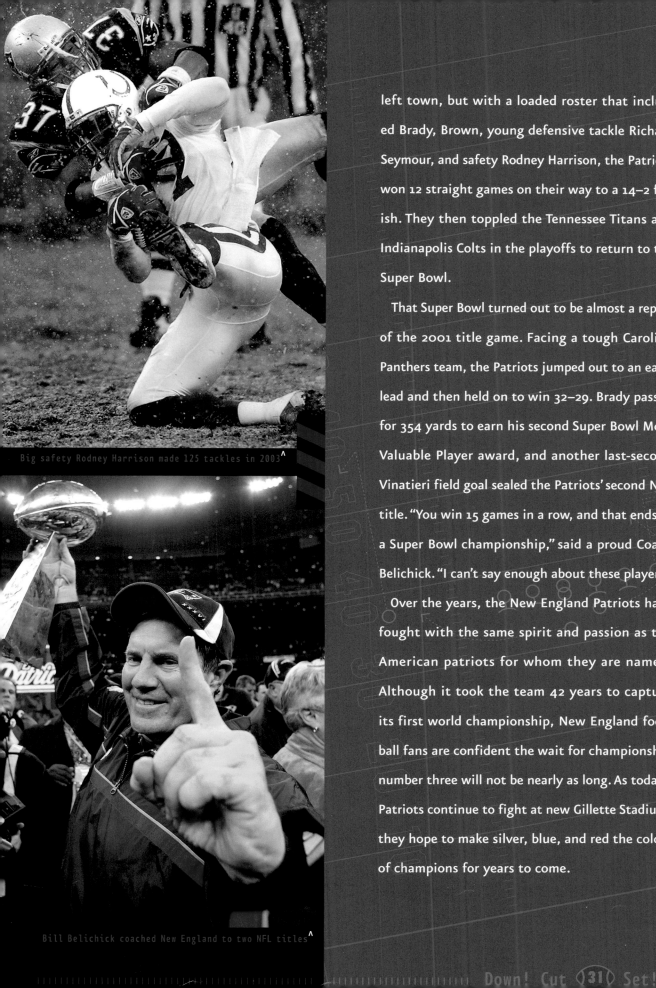

Big safety Rodney Harrison made 125 tackles in 2003 ^

Bill Belichick coached New England to two NFL titles ^

left town, but with a loaded roster that included Brady, Brown, young defensive tackle Richard Seymour, and safety Rodney Harrison, the Patriots won 12 straight games on their way to a 14–2 finish. They then toppled the Tennessee Titans and Indianapolis Colts in the playoffs to return to the Super Bowl.

That Super Bowl turned out to be almost a replay of the 2001 title game. Facing a tough Carolina Panthers team, the Patriots jumped out to an early lead and then held on to win 32–29. Brady passed for 354 yards to earn his second Super Bowl Most Valuable Player award, and another last-second Vinatieri field goal sealed the Patriots' second NFL title. "You win 15 games in a row, and that ends in a Super Bowl championship," said a proud Coach Belichick. "I can't say enough about these players."

Over the years, the New England Patriots have fought with the same spirit and passion as the American patriots for whom they are named. Although it took the team 42 years to capture its first world championship, New England football fans are confident the wait for championship number three will not be nearly as long. As today's Patriots continue to fight at new Gillette Stadium, they hope to make silver, blue, and red the colors of champions for years to come.

INDEX>